Wallykazam!™

By Kristen L. Depken

Based on the episode "Castle Caper" by Gabriel Pulliam

Illustrated by Cartobaleno

A Random House PICTUREBACK® Book

Random House 🏠 New York

© 2015 Viacom International Inc. All rights reserved. Published in the United States by Random House Children's Books, a division of Random House LLC, 1745 Broadway, New York, NY 10019, and in Canada by Random House of Canada Limited, Toronto, Penguin Random House Companies. Pictureback, Random House, and the Random House colophon are registered trademarks of Random House LLC. Nickelodeon, Wallykazam!, and all related titles, logos, and characters are trademarks of Viacom International Inc.

randomhousekids.com

ISBN 978-0-553-52313-3

MANUFACTURED IN CHINA

10 9 8 7 6 5 4 3 2 1

One day, Wally decided to do something really special for his pet dragon, Norville. It had to be something that started with the letter **c**, because that was the magic letter of the day.

Wally raised his magic stick and said, "Wallykazam! Wallykazastle! Magic Stick, make Norville a **castle**!" With that, a **castle** appeared. Norville was excited to go inside. Someone else was, too—Bobgoblin!

Norville loved the castle! But Wally thought it needed something else.

He waved his magic stick and made **couches** and **carpets** appear!

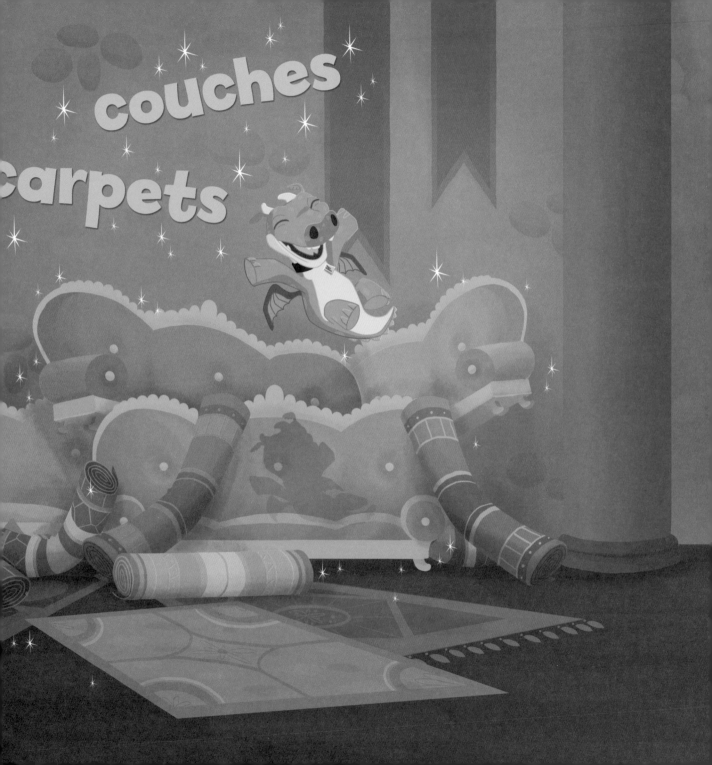

couches

carpets

crow

Gina Giant came to visit Wally and Norville.

"You're just in time!" said Wally. "I'm about to make Norville the king of the castle."

Wally waved his magic stick, and the word **king** popped out—but nothing happened!

"Oh, **king** starts with the letter **k**, not the letter **c**," Wally said. He waved his stick again. "Don't worry, Norville. I can make you the king if I make you a **crown**!"

A crown appeared, but just as it was about to land on Norville's head, Bobgoblin ran up—and the crown landed on his head instead!

"Bobgoblin has the crown, so that makes Bobgoblin the king!" said Bobgoblin. He ran into the castle and locked the doors.

Norville whimpered sadly.

"Don't worry, buddy," Wally told him. "That's still your castle, and you're still the king. We just have to find a way inside."

Wally hopped on Norville and they flew up to the castle's windows—but Bobgoblin shut and locked them all.
"No invaders! No dragons! No trolls!" shouted Bobgoblin, holding up his list of rules. When he saw Gina, he quickly added, "And no giants!"

no invaders
no dragons
no trolls

Bobgoblin lounged on Norville's couches.

He slid down the stairs on Norville's carpets.

He banged the royal pots and pans and even ate all the royal jam!

"Time for a new plan," said Wally. "Maybe we can sneak Norville into the castle without Bobgoblin noticing."

"You can hide Norville inside something!" said Gina.

Wally used his magic stick to make a **cake** for Norville to hide in!

To get the cake into the castle, Wally decided to disguise himself. He waved his magic stick, and he was suddenly in a cake-delivery **costume**.

"Ready, Norville?" Wally asked as he picked up the cake and headed for the castle doors.

Wally knocked on the door and tried to deliver the cake, but when Norville made a noise inside it, Bobgoblin figured out what was going on.

"No invaders, no dragons, no trolls, no giants, and no cakes!" said Bobgoblin, and he slammed the door.

Bobgoblin went out on the castle balcony and pulled a rope to ring the castle's bell.

"Hear ye, hear ye! Let the bell ring for King Bobgoblin!" he cried.

The ringing bell gave Wally an idea. "That's it!" he said. "Norville can fly into the castle through the bell tower. Gina and I just have to get Bobgoblin to look at us instead of Norville!"

So Wally and Gina began to dance for Bobgoblin. While he was watching them, Norville flew up to the bell tower.

But when Norville was halfway there, Bobgoblin spotted him. "Invader!" he shouted.

"Hurry, Norville!" cried Wally.

Norville flew as fast as he could while Bobgoblin raced up to the bell tower.

"I have to help him!" said Wally. Suddenly, he had an idea. He pulled out a book and showed Gina a picture in it. "We need that machine to fling me up to the castle!"

catapult

"I know what it is—a catapult!" said Gina. "It's a giant word."
"**Catapult** starts with the letter **c**!" Wally shouted. "So it's a magic word, too!"
Wally waved his magic stick, and a catapult appeared. He climbed into it.

Gina pulled the lever, and Wally went flying up, up, up into the air. He landed on Norville's back, and together they reached the bell tower before Bobgoblin.

"We did it! We're in the castle!" said Wally.

But they didn't realize that the bell tower didn't have a floor. Suddenly, they were falling!

"We just need something soft to land on!" said Wally. "Like **cushions**!" He waved his magic stick, and a pile of cushions appeared just in time.

A moment later, Bobgoblin also fell from the bell tower onto the cushions—and his crown popped off and landed on Norville's head!

"Invaders!" cried Bobgoblin.

"Bobgoblin, this is Norville's castle," explained Wally. "I made it just for him, so he is the king."

"Oh, well," said Bobgoblin. "Bobgoblin doesn't want a dragon castle. King Bobgoblin will find a goblin castle. Good day!" And he left!

"Norville, you're the king!" cried Gina. Norville took his place on the throne, and Wally and Gina bowed before him.

The castle and the crown belonged to King Norville.

© Viacom International Inc.

© Viacom International Inc.

© Viacom International Inc.

© Viacom International Inc.